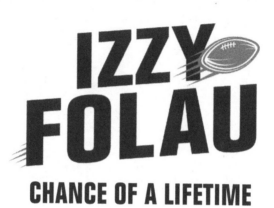

CHANCE OF A LIFETIME

IZZY FOLAU

CHANCE OF A LIFETIME

WRITTEN BY
DAVID HARDING
ILLUSTRATED BY
JAMES FOSDIKE

RANDOM HOUSE AUSTRALIA

A Random House book
Published by Random House Australia Pty Ltd
Level 3, 100 Pacific Highway, North Sydney NSW 2060
www.randomhouse.com.au

Penguin
Random House
RANDOM HOUSE BOOKS

First published by Random House Australia in 2015

Random House Books is part of the Penguin Random House group of
companies whose addresses can be found at global.penguinrandomhouse.com.

National Library of Australia
Cataloguing-in-Publication Entry

Creator: Harding, David, author
Title: Chance of a lifetime/David Harding and Israel Folau; illustrated by James Fosdike
ISBN: 978 0 85798 661 0 (pbk)
Series: Izzy Folau; 1
Target Audience: For primary school age
Subjects: Rugby Union football players – Australia – Juvenile fiction.
          Rugby football coaches – Australia – Juvenile fiction.
          Rugby football – Coaching – Australia – Juvenile fiction.
          Rugby Union football – Australia – Juvenile fiction.
Other creators/contributors: Folau, Israel, author; Fosdike, James, illustrator
Dewey number: A823.4

Illustrations by James Fosdike
Front cover image of Israel Folau by Chris Hyde/Getty Images
Back cover image of Israel Folau by Matt King/Getty Images
Cover design by Christabella Designs
Internal design and typesetting by Midland Typesetters, Australia
Printed in Australia by Griffin Press, an accredited ISO AS/NZS 14001:2004
Environmental Management System printer

DANIEL

BAM! The forwards slammed into the scrum machine. It creaked and rocked backwards as the eight boys in their deep-green rugby jerseys pushed against it with all their might.

'Whoa, whoa! Hold it!' Mr Richards shouted. The boys relaxed and stood up, watching as their coach lowered one of the thick pads on the front of the scrum machine. Daniel watched him and waited.

The scrum machine wasn't really a machine so much as a huge bulk of metal arms that held soft padding at shoulder level. By pushing against it, the forwards were practising how to form a scrum with an opposing team, just like on game day.

To finish that afternoon's training session, Mr Richards had wanted the boys to practise getting the ball from the scrum to the distant wing as quickly as possible. Daniel, the team's captain and fly-half, knew exactly what he needed to do. If only the forwards would hurry up and get their act together.

'All right, one more time,' Mr Richards said.

The forwards put their arms around each other, bent down and slammed into the machine, panting and grunting. The scrum-half fed the ball to the scrum by throwing it into their collection of feet. The ball came out the back and he expertly passed it to Daniel. Daniel ran forward a few steps, imagining the opposition charging towards him, before shooting the ball to the inside centre. From there, the ball zipped all the way down the line of backs that were spread out across the field, ending up in the hands of the winger on the far side. He put the ball down over the tryline, signalling the end of another sweaty training session.

'Well done!' Mr Richards shouted, clapping his hands enthusiastically, then waved for his team to gather in front of him. Once the players sat on the ground, the coach continued. 'Great work today, boys. We're starting to remove those kinks in our back line. Remember to watch Daniel – he's the key. As soon as that ball is fed, you should be watching and ready, but don't move off your line early.'

'No, sir,' the boys replied.

'Right, well, the last game of the season will be our toughest – everyone knows that – but St Martin's are the only thing standing between us and an undefeated season, and I know we'll be ready on Saturday.'

'Green. And. WHITE! Green. And. WHITE!' the boys chanted in response.

'Now, before you go home, I have some good news and some bad news.' Mr Richards looked behind him and saw that most of the boys' parents were now waiting in the distance. 'The bad news isn't unexpected – Johnno still hasn't fully recovered from his tonsillitis, so William will be in the centre – no big deal, we'll be fine . . .'

Daniel sat in the grass, watching the late-winter sun slowly disappear behind a grey cloud. He shivered with excitement, anticipating what was coming next.

'But now for the good news,' Mr Richards announced.

Daniel looked up at his coach's face and their eyes met.

'Daniel, could you come up here, please?'

It's actually happening, Daniel thought, glancing over at his dad. He walked around his teammates' sprawled legs and stood next to Mr Richards. 'We all know about the rep team – how the selectors were here to watch us play. Well, this morning I received a telephone call advising me that our very own Daniel has been selected to play for the Valley rep team at the State Championships in a few weeks.'

The other boys cheered and clapped. Whoops echoed around the field. But, best of all, Daniel could hear his dad shouting congratulations from two hundred metres away.

Mr Richards smiled. 'I was also informed that the team will be going on a two-week tour before the Championships begin, and that the team will be coached by . . .'

Izzy Folau! Izzy Folau! Daniel repeated over

and over in his mind, wishing it might actually be his all-time favourite rugby player.

'Israel Folau!'

The team clapped and cheered again as Daniel's jaw hung open. 'What! Really?' he said. 'Are you serious, sir?'

'You bet!' Mr Richards shook Daniel's hand. 'You'll be getting your rep jersey at tomorrow's assembly. Congratulations, I'm sure you will do Barton Grammar proud.'

'Yes, sir,' Daniel answered before he was mobbed by his team. All the boys slapped him on the back and said how jealous they were of him. Daniel tried to soak it all up, but he was in shock to think that he was going to be coached by the greatest of the greats – Izzy Folau.

Soon enough, the cheers died down and one by one the others walked off the oval until Daniel was the only player left on the field. He looked up at the gigantic goalposts and tried to settle his thoughts.

This was a big deal. It wasn't just the fact that he was going on a trip with Izzy Folau. Daniel knew that being selected for the rep team was the first step to becoming a Wallaby himself. It was all he'd ever wanted. Now, just as his dad had predicted many times, his dreams were starting to come true.

Daniel picked up the football from near the touchline, along with his kicking tee. He decided to start with a hard one. He put the kicking tee at the corner of the touchline and the 22-yard line. He looked at the goalposts and exhaled slowly. It would be hard to get the distance let alone the angle, but he wanted to try. He thought back to just days before, when he'd watched Izzy being interviewed on TV after a loss.

'We tried our best,' Izzy had said. 'We didn't win, but we gave it our best shot and that's what matters most.'

Daniel sighed, remembering how his dad had grunted when he'd heard Izzy say that. He'd called it 'loser talk'. Daniel looked at the posts again. Whether he kicked the goal or not, he wanted to give it a go – just like Izzy – no matter what his dad thought about him.

He considered the ball and sniffed it. The smell of a rugby ball always made him smile. He flicked the ball into the air, making it spin briskly as it popped upwards before falling back into his hands. He flicked it again, watching as it seemed to hang in the air, almost magically.

A voice echoed across the empty grounds, shaking him from his thoughts. 'Daniel! It's goal-kicking practice, not time-wasting practice. Let's go!'

He turned to see his dad watching him, his phone pressed to his ear as always. Daniel nodded and put the ball on the tee before measuring his run-up. He stood at his spot, breathing deeply. He looked at the ball, then at the goalposts and back at the ball, imagining how best to kick it. He replayed the goal kick twenty times in his imagination before going for it. Finally, he jogged towards the

ball, balanced his body and let his foot force-fully yet gently connect with it.

It was a great goal.

His dad clapped on his knee from the stands, and Daniel smiled his biggest smile since Christmas as he ran after the ball. The rep team, the tour *and* Izzy Folau – it was almost too good to be true.

SIONE

Sione lay on his bed, holding his football. It was hardly white anymore. He thought back to when he'd first got it, before all the scratches and scuff marks, to his birthday over six months ago, and smiled. He'd been so excited, even though the gift wasn't a surprise at all. He remembered his aunt handing him

13

the football-shaped present and laughing about how hard it had been to wrap. It hadn't mattered to Sione, though. He'd been so grateful for the ball that he'd actually hugged Aunty. And that was probably the first time he had ever hugged her – or anyone, really.

He flicked the ball above his head, watching it spin in the air for that split second as it hovered. It was almost like magic.

For the millionth time, Sione wished he could fly like a football. That way, he'd be able to go wherever he wanted, whenever he wanted. When things got tough, he could just rise above it and hide in the clouds for a while.

Sione kept throwing the ball into the air, remembering the first time he'd thrown it, and the squeal he had let out when it landed

in mud. The other Tigers had laughed at him then. They'd thought it was hilarious that Sione should treat his new ball like a newborn baby. But of course he would – it was special.

Now, each splat of mud or scratch from a football boot was like a badge of honour, a mark that told a story of an amazing try or a thumping tackle.

Lost in his daydream, Sione missed catching his ball and it bounced across his bedroom floor. He sighed and rolled over, his eyes coming to rest on the Izzy Folau poster taped to his wall. The Wallaby was smiling wide and running across ANZ Stadium, on his way to a match-winning try beneath the posts.

Sione had studied that poster so often that he'd invented names for all the tiny specks of faces that he could see in the crowd behind Izzy. He could smell the wet grass, he could feel a thumping in his chest. He wished he was on the Australian team, running alongside Izzy.

The phone in the kitchen rang, and Sione could hear his dad walking towards it. Those footsteps were unmistakable; the heavy work boots almost shaking the house as he walked, unlike his little sister's *slap-slap-slapping* across the floorboards, or his aunt's quiet padding.

Sione couldn't make out the words but it was a long conversation. That meant it wasn't a salesperson. It was probably a relative, or maybe even his mum. Sione closed his eyes tight, trying to lift his body off the bed and into the clouds with the power of his mind.

'Sione!' his dad called.

Sione's eyes snapped open and he sat up.

'Sione! Get your butt out here!'

He stood up as his little sister's slapping footsteps approached at double speed.

Mele burst into the bedroom and tugged at her brother's rugby shorts. 'Sione's butt! Sione's butt!' she sang, pushing him into the hall.

'Okay, okay, I'm coming!' Sione followed Mele into the kitchen, where their dad stood, leaning on the counter, his back to them. His dad had the usual dirt marks all over his legs and was wearing his neon-green work shirt.

Sione wondered if each of the marks told a story like the ones on his football did.

His dad turned around, looking exhausted as usual. He stared at Sione without saying anything. Mele ran up to his dirty, hairy legs and he swung her up in one swift movement.

'Sione . . .'

Sione braced himself for what sounded like bad news. But the fact that his dad wasn't shouting meant he wasn't in trouble. *So what is it?* he thought to himself.

'That was Terry,' his dad continued. 'Sione . . .'

What's wrong? Why is it so hard for him to spit it out? Have I been kicked off the team?

'Son, you've been picked for the rep team.'

'The rep team?' Sione repeated.

'The Valley team. You've been selected to play for Valley at the State Championships!'

It took Sione a moment for his brain to register what he was hearing, and then he remembered. His coach, Terry, had put some names forward to the selection committee; selectors had even come to watch the Tigers train and play a game. But Sione hadn't given it another thought – he'd never dreamed he would be selected.

'Why me?' he said. 'I'm not even good enough to play for Valley.'

'Don't be so down on yourself, Si,' his dad said, lowering Mele to the ground. 'You're good.'

Those words echoed around the kitchen as if it were a cave. No matter how many times he heard them, he would never believe it.

'If I'm so good, why aren't you smiling?' Sione asked.

His dad sighed. 'Before the Championship weekend, the Valley team is going on a two-week tour. They'll train together, play other teams from around the country, do all this team-building stuff. Oh, and Izzy Folau will be their coach.'

'What?!'

'Each team in the state has been assigned a famous player to coach them, and apparently Valley got Izzy.'

This is amazing! By the end of the two weeks I'll be best friends with my favourite player of all time!

'Are you kidding me?' Sione said. 'That's awesome!'

His dad shook his head. 'It's true, but the thing is . . . most of what you need is covered – they give you the uniforms and the kit – but each player's family has to cover the cost of sending you on the trip around the country and, well . . .' Sione's dad leant against the kitchen counter. He didn't finish his sentence – he didn't need to.

Sione fought back tears, turning his eyes into brick walls that nothing could pass through. He was good at doing that – hiding his emotions. It was something he had done many times.

Why did Terry put my name down for this? he thought, clenching his fists and looking away from his dad.

An unexpected noise sounded as the front doorknob clicked and turned before Sione's aunt bustled in.

'You'll never guess what —' She stopped mid-stride as she stared at her brother and nephew standing silently in the kitchen. 'What's wrong?' she asked, placing a bag of groceries on the floor.

Sione looked up at her, his face burning.

'What is it, Sione?' she asked.

He screwed up his eyes, trying to respond without letting a tear fall. When he finally spoke, his voice was cracked and high-pitched.

'I got selected for the rugby rep team,' he said. With that, he walked down the hall, slammed his bedroom door and collapsed onto his bed.

DANIEL

Friday assemblies were usually the most boring thing on earth. The school hall was a large, cavernous room that became hot and stuffy when a thousand boys crammed in after lunch each week. Daniel and his friends always tried to sit in one of the back corners, out of sight from teachers, where they could whisper about their next rugby match. Today, Daniel sat right in the middle of the assembly hall, where the headmaster would be looking in his direction the whole time, but Daniel didn't care. This assembly was going to be sweet.

Once the hall was full, the school captain called for everyone to rise. The headmaster and deputy principal walked in, up the stage steps and stood facing the students, awaiting the national anthem.

Soon, I'll be up there too, Daniel thought.

He usually couldn't be bothered singing the anthem, but today he sang each word loud and clear. His friends on either side of him did the same. They all stood straight and tall, proud of Daniel and the fact that he – now destined for great things — was their friend. Knowing this made Daniel sing even louder.

His best friend, Steve, glanced over and laughed. 'What's up with you, Mr Opera Singer?'

Eventually, the headmaster announced the big news that Daniel Masters had made the rugby rep team. The entire crowd of students broke out into applause in a way Daniel had never heard. He couldn't help but grin as he walked down his row and out into the aisle, lapping up the attention.

Everyone was still clapping as he stepped onto the stage. Barton Grammar prided itself on rugby, and Daniel was now one of its stars. Mr Richards appeared from somewhere back-stage and was holding a roll of green material that Daniel assumed was his new rep jersey. *Green — just like Barton's colours*, he thought to himself.

It felt so foreign to be up there, but Daniel was loving every second of it. A thousand faces were looking at him. He could only just make out his empty chair in the middle of the hall.

Mr Richards leant in to the microphone. 'It gives me great pleasure to present Daniel with this jersey. I am proud of all he has accomplished this season; his representative selection is well deserved. I know that he will represent Valley — and Barton Grammar — as brilliantly as anyone can.'

He then shook Daniel's hand as Mr Varnes, the school photographer, snapped away.

The jersey unravelled, and Mr Richards and Daniel each held up one shoulder and sleeve of the precious garment as more photos were taken. Daniel didn't think his cheeks could handle much more smiling.

'And now,' the headmaster said to the school, 'I would like to read out an email that we received this morning from Israel Folau, the Valley team's coach.'

Excited whispers filled the hall.

'Congratulations, Daniel,' the headmaster read aloud, 'on your selection to the Valley team. I can't wait to meet you and start training together in preparation for the State Championships.' Daniel's chest puffed out and his hands grew clammy. 'Every time I have faced a new challenge, I have felt anxious and unsure, but also extremely excited. I hope you are pleased with your selection and are looking forward to all the fun we will have as a team. Izzy.'

The headmaster nodded at the school captain, who shouted, 'Three cheers for Daniel. Hip hip!'

'Hooray!' the school chorused.

'Hip hip!'

'Hooray!'

'Hip hip!'

'Hooray!'

Daniel threw his schoolbag onto the back seat of his father's car and jumped in.

'Congratulations!' his dad said, looking back at him from the driver's seat. 'It's really happening, huh?'

The car pulled out from the school's kiss-and-drop zone and Daniel put on his seatbelt, making sure not to crease his jersey.

'What happened at the assembly?'

'Not much,' Daniel answered. 'Everyone clapped and Mr Richards shook my hand.'

'Nice!'

'The headmaster read out a letter from Izzy.'

'Really?' his dad said. 'What did it say?'

Daniel shrugged. 'Just that we're going to have fun and stuff.'

'Hmm.'

'What?'

'I would have thought that a coach – of a *youth* rep team, especially – would be all about geeing up his players to be the best they can be on the field,' Daniel's father said. 'His job is to toughen you up and show you how to win at the highest level. You don't need to be shown how to have fun – winning *is* fun!'

Daniel had heard all of this before and knew it wasn't worth disagreeing, so he just said nothing.

The rest of the car ride was silent except for the couple of times his dad asked about the game against St Martin's the next day. Daniel had actually forgotten all about the match, as important as it was. Somehow, in the past twenty-four hours, tomorrow's game had gone from being the final and possibly record-breaking match of the season to a non-event. Now that he was on the rep team, how he performed seemed irrelevant. Daniel sighed. Maybe he would try doing what Izzy had talked about and just have some fun.

After picking Daniel up from school, Mr Masters always went back to work for a couple of hours. For Daniel, this usually meant homework time – but not on Fridays. On Fridays he was allowed to practise his goal kicking in the park.

Daniel got out of the car and ran to get changed into his training gear. He neatly folded the rep jersey and placed it on his pillow. He paused, thinking how that would have made his mum smile. Then he gathered up a ball, his house keys and a water bottle and was gone, jogging down the street to the only place he ever truly felt at home.

SIONE

'Izzy grabs the ball and runs hard, sidestepping one defender, pushing away another, and passes the ball just before he's taken out. It's a beautiful cut-out pass that skips the centre and lands in the hands of the winger. Izzy falls on the ground with his arms outstretched. It's a try!'

The other players picked up Izzy and brushed the dirt off him, cheering and hollering. Lunchtimes at Valley North Primary School were always the same. Fifteen to thirty boys would gather on the grass to play touch footy while teachers supervised, ensuring little kids weren't getting trampled. Lately, Sam, who had broken his leg, would commentate, hobbling along on his crutches, trying to keep up with the play. The other boys had said that the commentary had made their games feel more real, like on TV, and so they had started pretending they were Wallabies. The only problem was that everyone seemed to want to be Israel Folau.

'There's the tap to restart play,' Sam shouted from the middle of the field. 'Izzy takes it a few metres before passing the ball to Izzy. Izzy passes it to Izzy, down the back line it goes. They're trying to keep it from the opposition, who are coming in fast. And Izzy has kicked the ball, high and for touch. It does go out, but almost immediately. The team has only made about ten metres all up.'

Sione sighed and braced himself for his team's comments. He had kicked an absolute shocker. But no one said anything. He quickly got into position to wait for the line-out that would bring the ball back into play, as anxious thoughts swirled around in his mind. *How did the rep selectors get it so wrong? Why had they put him in this situation of being selected but unable to go?* Sione wished they'd never selected him in the first place.

The ball bounced clumsily over the hands and heads of ten or so Izzys, all scrambling to gain control of the ball, before it landed in the grip of one of the boys on Sione's team. The boys weren't allowed to play tackle, so as soon as that boy was touched by a defender he had to stop. He tapped the ball on his foot and passed it to Sione. He wasn't really expecting it and so didn't have time to think about what he would do next. Somehow, he slipped his body between two defending Izzys and was clear. He ran hard alongside the touchline for about twenty metres, until he was past the tryline. He put the ball down. The whole thing had seemed to take about two seconds.

Sione turned to see everyone looking at him with their eyes wide and their jaws hanging open. Sam had even stopped commentating. *What have I done now?* Sione thought.

'Um, how did you do that?' Sam asked.

Sione shrugged his shoulders. Strange things like that happened when he played for the Tigers, too, and Sione had no idea why or how.

'Those two guys were right in front of you,' Sam said. 'How did you get through them without even being touched?'

'I dunno,' Sione replied softly.

'That happened in our match last week, too,' Thomas, a Tigers player, said. 'Our coach calls Sione "Eel" because he can slip through the defence line like that. Before they even realise he's through, he's gone.'

The bell rang, signalling the end of lunch.

Sione breathed a sigh of relief, glad to have the attention off him.

The boys trudged up the hill from the back of the school, towards the concrete playground and the row of bubblers that looked so inviting after all their running around. But going as quickly as Sam could manage on his crutches meant that by the time they got to have a drink, Sione and his friends were the only students left in sight – everyone else was lining up outside their classrooms.

'Sione Taito!' Ms Collier, the deputy principal, boomed from across the deserted playground. 'I'd like to speak to you for a moment, please.'

The boys froze. They had been caught getting back to class late. Sione felt sick.

His dad wouldn't be happy when he learnt that Sione had got in trouble at school.

Ms Collier walked over to the group. 'The rest of you, hurry back to class and tell Sione's teacher he's with me.'

'Yes, Ms Collier,' the boys said, glancing back at Sione a couple of times to try to judge the level of strife he was in.

Sione stared at his feet. The deputy was tall and imposing, like the Year 12 rugby players who pushed past him at the train station and who stormed onto the training field before his team had finished every Tuesday night.

'You're not in trouble,' Ms Collier said, but Sione still didn't look up. The gritty asphalt below his feet went blurry. 'Congratulations on your rugby selection,' she added, before handing him a white piece of paper folded neatly in half. He reached for it slowly but didn't open it.

'It's an email from Israel Folau, just for you,' she said. 'Read it – I think you'll like it.'

Sione smiled, but stopped when he saw Ms Collier watching him. He couldn't wait for this conversation to be finished so he could read the email in private.

After a moment, seemingly resigned to the fact that she wasn't going to get a word out of him, Ms Collier got to the big news. 'I've been talking to your coach and the principal, and we've had an idea. It would be a shame for you to miss the rugby tour; I understand the costs of it are a little high.'

Sione swallowed, his cheeks burning.

'We'd like to announce a mufti day in your honour for this Monday. Every student will be allowed to wear their favourite jersey or team colours instead of the school uniform, the cost being a gold-coin donation towards your travel expenses. I know it isn't much notice, but hopefully all the students will be able to bring some money to help you out. Lots of gold coins can really add up.'

Sione said nothing. He couldn't decide if he felt excited or embarrassed by the whole thing.

'What do you think? Can I call your dad to let him know?'

Sione nodded, and Ms Collier excused herself and left. Immediately, Sione's stomach lurched. He hated that feeling. He wanted to be a part of the Valley rep team more than anything, but not at the cost of becoming the centre of attention. How could he ask all the kids at school to give him money? What if he did get to go on the tour but played terribly? Then he'd be *wasting* everyone's money.

Sione trudged back to his classroom. He walked even slower once he heard the maths lesson that was taking place inside. He tucked Izzy's email safely inside his pocket and went in, face down.

The rest of that afternoon was a haze. At one point, prefects came in to announce the mufti day and even mentioned something about Sione making a speech at the Monday assembly. As everyone in his class talked about what they would wear, Sione's stomach sank.

He didn't want to get up in front of the entire school, let alone speak in front of them.

By the time Sione arrived home, he'd decided he wasn't going to school on Monday. This rep team thing was getting way too big.

On Sunday, Sione lay in bed all evening with his stomach in knots. He listened as his family ate dinner without him, frequently punctuated by his dad bursting out with: 'But he'll miss his own mufti day!'

Sione looked up at the giant poster of Izzy on his wall, and at some point he fell asleep. He slept long but far from deeply. When he got out of bed in the morning his dad had already left for work. Aunty and Mele were eating toast in the kitchen.

'How are you this morning, dear?' his aunt asked.

Sione looked at the clock on the microwave. It was nine o'clock, too late to get to school. 'A bit better,' he replied.

'Would you like some toast?'

Sione nodded.

'It's a good sign that you feel like eating again,' his aunt said, getting up.

Mele was bopping up and down in her booster seat as music played in the next room. Sione smiled but was careful not to look too happy. He grimaced and held his stomach when Aunty put the toast in front of him.

'You know,' she said, 'I saw Israel Folau on TV last night.'

Sione looked down at his breakfast, but his ears perked upwards like a cat's at the mention of Izzy's name.

'He was talking about how he's changed sports twice and all the challenges he'd faced doing that, like having to learn new things and meet new people and be on the news every night.' She paused, waiting for a reaction from Sione. 'Anyway, he seems like a great guy. I hope you do get to meet him. I'm proud of anyone who faces their problems rather than hiding or running away.'

Sione coughed on his breakfast, and his aunty got him some milk to drink.

That day, as the kids at school dressed in his honour, Sione read Izzy's email over and over again. What's more, he stuck it on his wall above his bed, right next to the poster, so he might dream about it all night.

If Izzy can do tough things, he told himself, *maybe I can too.*

SIONE

The mufti day turned out to be a success, with the money covering the travel costs. Soon after, Sione received his rep jersey and all the details for the training camp and tour. A week later, Sione found himself standing at the bus stop by the train station with his family, waiting for the bus to take him away for his two-week training camp and then the statewide Junior Rugby Championships.

It was a sunny Saturday morning – winter was clearly on the way out – but Sione couldn't appreciate it. His family was sitting at the bus stop, laughing about something or other while Sione stood as stiff as a board next to the bus-stop sign, refusing to sit with them. There was no way he was missing this bus after all that had happened.

He stared down the open road, and it occurred to him that he wasn't anxious about spending two weeks away from home, rather, he was afraid of getting found out. He was sure that, as soon as training started, everyone would see that he was a fake. Hopefully he would be picked to sit on the reserve bench for every game. Then his talent levels would never be in question, or even required.

I haven't even played rugby in two weeks, he thought to himself as he looked down the road. *I'll stink.*

The bus was going to take Sione and the other selected boys to a conference centre, an hour's drive towards the city. They were to spend three days there, getting to know each other and train under Izzy, before going to the airport late on Monday. After that there would be the tour matches across the country before landing back in his home state – this year's host for the Championships.

Sione's aunt had said over and over again how much fun he was going to have and how lucky he was to visit all those places. Sione's dad had said he wished he could go in Sione's place, and Sione was very tempted to let him.

Sione thought about his schoolmates. They were just starting their school holidays and could spend the next two weeks lounging around at home, relaxing, while he was being forced to go on an adventure. He felt exhausted already.

He leant against the bus-stop sign, watching the road. Suddenly, a square speck appeared on the horizon. It grew and grew until it was clear that the team bus was exactly what it was. Aunty stood up, holding Mele's hand, and Dad followed them to stand next to Sione. Now he wasn't just stressed, he was embarrassed, too. He doubted the other boys would have had their families wait with them like they were little kids.

Aunty hugged Sione, and his dad rubbed his head with his rough workman's hand.

As the bus approached, Sione's mind raced through a hundred different escape options and what people might say if he actually did just turn and run. Then he looked at his aunt and remembered what she had said about Izzy and facing challenges instead of running away. He tightened his fists and stood tall. *I'm going to do this*, he decided. *I'm going to face it and do well. If Izzy can, so can . . . Izzy? Is Israel Folau going to be on this bus?* Sione felt like vomiting all over again.

Mele clapped as the bus slowed to a stop, its brakes hissing. It was a very large coach, painted an ominous black. Sione looked upwards, towards the muffled sound of excited boys. It was hard to see well through the tinted windows, but Sione could make out fingers pressed against the glass, pointing in his direction.

Sione groaned inwardly. He lowered his head and turned to face the front door as it whooshed open. His family gathered around him but Sione didn't move.

A sneaker appeared on the steps of the bus. It was followed by a leg in track pants and a Wallabies polo shirt. Above the shirt was a face that bore a smile that Sione knew only too well. He had traced its outlines and features with his eyes every night before going to bed. His poster had come to life.

Sione's aunt gasped as Israel Folau walked towards them. He headed straight for Sione and held out his hand. 'Hi, you must be Sione,' he said with a smile.

Mele giggled, peering from her hiding spot behind one of Sione's legs. Izzy bent his head to see her and waved, causing her to giggle again. Sione didn't know what to say or do. Mele nudged him and pointed to Izzy's hand, which was still hanging in the air. Sione quickly grasped it, shaking Izzy's hand gently.

Izzy grinned. 'Welcome to the team!'

Sione nodded, trying to think of what to say. 'G-Good morning, Mr Folau.'

'Call me Izzy.'

'Uh, o-okay . . . Izzy.' Sione blinked.

Some other adults wearing the team training gear introduced themselves to Sione's dad and aunt. They were in charge of the tour and looking after the boys but Sione didn't catch their names. His dad handed over some medical forms and emergency phone numbers, and before Sione knew it, he was being squeezed goodbye once again by his aunt and sister. One tear did make it through his eye's defences this time. He was going to miss them. Not just because he loved his family, but because they were familiar and safe.

Izzy directed Sione to the door of the bus after the driver had packed his luggage in the storage bay next to its large wheels. Sione's stomach turned again – he didn't want to go in. *What will the boys think of me?* he wondered.

Gingerly, without a backwards glance, he walked up the steps and stood at the front of the bus, scanning the space as a dozen or more pairs of eyes looked back at him. He spotted a seat by the window and imagined swinging his backpack onto the rack above it and hiding himself behind his headphones, alone, until they got to the camp.

But then Izzy climbed the steps behind Sione and spoke to the bus full of kids. 'Everyone, this is Sione. He plays wing for Valley.'

All the other boys immediately began to holler and stamp their feet. The tour leaders behind Sione started clapping their welcome, and soon the whole bus filled with the sound of applause.

Just like that, Sione felt like a part of the team.

DANIEL

Daniel sat at the bus stop, trying to tune out his dad, who had spent the past hour going on and on about what an important day this was and how it was a stepping stone towards Daniel playing for Australia. It wasn't that Daniel didn't agree with him, it was just that he was trying to focus.

Last year, a sports psychologist had visited the school and given a talk at assembly. He'd said it was important to stay focused in all areas of life – school and sport. The psychologist had talked about what some famous athletes did before a big match to get themselves in the zone.

Many sports stars listen to music before a game to keep calm, or have a very specific warm-up routine. Some of them even do yoga. Daniel had decided the music option was the one for him. It would keep him focused as he thought about the big two weeks in front of him and all he had to prove. Plus, he'd look so cool walking onto the bus while holding the latest phone. But his dad had said it was rude to have headphones on while someone was talking to you, so the phone was in his pocket.

Daniel knew that from the moment he sat down in the bus, he wanted to be the leader, not a follower. He was certain that his rugby prowess made him ready for the job as a representative player, but projecting himself into the role of captain – *that* would be what would set him apart on this tour.

'Just don't forget that this isn't the end of the road,' his dad said. 'The job of the selectors is never over. They'll be watching this team, too, looking for the players they think will best represent the entire state at the end of the year. You'll have to fight for your spot on that team every year until you're an adult and aiming for the Wallabies.'

Daniel nodded absently. He had heard this speech a hundred times. Every night at dinner his dad would talk to him about leadership and playing for the Wallabies and everything else. Daniel loved hearing he was destined for greatness, but he'd heard all his dad had to say already. He hoped that Israel Folau might be able to mentor him in a more direct manner.

Daniel thought back to the assembly the week before and the email from Izzy that the headmaster had read out. What Izzy had said about having fun excited him. It was a refreshing change from what he usually heard.

'Here it comes!'

Daniel stood up as soon as his dad spoke, and approached the kerb. The coach was large and black, with dark, tinted windows. It looked to Daniel like an enormous limo and that made him feel special. He could see excited boys peering out at him and pointing in his direction.

'It seems your fame has preceded you,' his dad laughed.

Daniel walked up to the front door as it opened. His dad wished him good luck and Daniel put his foot on the bottom step. Looking up, he saw the great Israel Folau walking down the few steps to meet him.

'Hi,' Izzy said with a smile. 'You must be Daniel.'

'That's me,' Daniel replied.

'Welcome to the tour,' Izzy said. 'It's so great to have you!'

Daniel smiled back at his idol. 'Thanks.'

'You can get on the bus if you like. I just need to introduce the staff to your dad.'

Daniel decided to step back off the coach to watch Izzy and three other adults in the Valley gear come out to shake hands with his dad.

'Nice to meet you, Israel,' his dad said.

'You too, but please call me Izzy.' They shook hands, and Izzy introduced the others as Daniel looked on, one hand on the bus's doorhandle. 'This is Jeremy Fisk. He's the tour manager, getting us everywhere we need to go to on time. This is Tom and Mary Parker, who will be looking after all the boys' needs. They'll be the ones who'll call you if we need anything.'

'Fine, fine, nice to meet you,' Daniel's dad said briskly. He pointed at his son. 'He's some player. You'll be amazed at what he can do.'

Mr Fisk smiled and nodded. 'Every boy that was selected was chosen because they have special talents.'

'Not quite like Daniel's, I'm sure,' Mr Masters countered. He waved goodbye as Daniel climbed onto the bus and put on his headphones.

'Everyone,' Izzy announced at the top of the stairs, 'this is Daniel. He plays fly-half for Valley. He's a great goal kicker, too.' Everyone clapped and cheered, and Daniel nodded. It seemed that they all loved him already. This was going to be sweet.

The seats on the coach were in rows, two seats on either side of the aisle. They had high backs, curtains at the windows and reading lights. It was almost as good as a plane.

Daniel chose the chair behind Izzy so he could get close to his new coach right from the start. He put his bag on the luggage rack above and settled into his chair with his music playing soft enough that he could still hear everything.

Some boys were chatting up the back but otherwise it was a very quiet bus. Daniel assumed it was because no one knew each other. He looked across the aisle and saw another boy sitting just like him, headphones on, minding his own business. The bus moved out of the bus stop and Izzy announced that there were only three more players to collect before heading off to the conference centre.

There were a few small TVs hanging from the ceiling at various points and a movie the boys had been watching flicked back on. Some were watching it intently, but Daniel ignored it. He had to focus.

Daniel looked back at the other boy, sizing him up. He was tall and thin, probably a winger. Daniel racked his brain for a way to begin a conversation with Izzy, who was now sitting just centimetres away.

Izzy turned, but instead of talking to Daniel, he called out to the other boy across from him. 'Sione!' he said. The boy turned his head cautiously. 'Tongan?' The boy called Sione smiled and nodded. 'Me too,' Izzy said.

'Yeah – I know,' Sione replied sheepishly.

Izzy turned back to look out the window and so did Sione. Daniel sank low in his seat. He was behind in the score already.

'Um, excuse me, Israel,' he said through the seats.

'Izzy,' came the reply with a chuckle.

'I just wanted to say thank you for the email you sent. My headmaster read it out at assembly. I thought it was great.'

Izzy turned to face Daniel over the back of his seat. 'My pleasure. I'm glad you liked it. It would be great to win, all I can ask is that we do our best and enjoy ourselves along the way.'

Daniel nodded. This was awesome! Izzy was awesome!

The bus pulled to another stop, and as Izzy and the other adults welcomed the next player to the team, the rest of the boys started chatting, looking through their windows and pointing. Some were guessing what position the new boy outside played.

'Flanker,' a boy said. 'We've only got one so far. Or second row, maybe.'

Daniel stood up to look at him. He knelt on the seat next to Sione and peered over his shoulder. He saw a regular-looking boy standing next to his parents, talking to Izzy and the others. Then the boy's mother bent over and kissed him on the cheek. Daniel laughed. This made Sione look up at him.

'Your mum doesn't still kiss you, does she?' he asked. When he didn't get a reply, Daniel shrugged his shoulders and returned to his seat.

The new boy climbed on the bus with Izzy, who announced, 'Hey guys, this is Tim. He plays second row and I hear he is a great goal kicker, too.'

Everyone clapped and cheered loudly, except for Daniel, who didn't make a sound. *Another goal kicker?* he fumed. *And the clapping is for everyone?*

Hunching down in his seat, Daniel turned up the volume and glared out the window.

SIONE

Music blared in Sione's ears as he read Izzy's email for the hundredth time. He still couldn't believe that Izzy had taken the time to write to him. Over the past week he had taken to reading the letter whenever he felt sad or anxious. Somehow it made him feel special, knowing that one of the greatest rugby players in the world knew who he was.

He looked over at Izzy sitting diagonally in front of him, and chuckled to himself. He was still so excited by Izzy's letter that he hadn't fully taken in the fact that Izzy himself was riding on the same bus!

The boy across the aisle shot him a quizzical look. His face seemed to say, 'What's up with you?', before he looked down at his pockets and began emptying them onto the seat next to him.

Chocolate after chocolate, lolly after lolly appeared, and by the time he was done there was a pyramid the size of which the ancient Egyptians would have been proud of. The boy rummaged through his pile until he found the bag of lollies he was looking for.

Sione couldn't help but watch. He hadn't

even thought to bring any junk food, wanting to look healthy in front of Izzy. This boy, on the other hand, seemed to be taking pride in all that he had.

The boy noticed Sione watching and sighed. Reluctantly, he held out his bag. 'Want one?' he asked.

Sione didn't. The taste of toothpaste was still in his mouth and he didn't think its mintiness would mix well with the sour cola lollies he was being offered. But he took one anyway and said thank you so as not to hurt the boy's feelings.

'What do you play?' the boy asked next.

Sione, struggling to enjoy the rubbery lolly, answered though glassy eyes and clenched teeth. 'Rugby.'

'I know that!' the boy snorted. 'I meant, what position do you play?'

Sione blushed. 'Wing.'

'Are you a goal kicker as well?'

'No.'

'That's good.' The boy smiled. 'I think it's bad for morale to have too many people try out for the same positions.' He swallowed a mouthful of lollies without flinching and said, 'My name's Daniel. I play fly-half.'

'I'm Sione. I play wing.'

'Yeah, you already said that.'

Sione knew that the rules of conversation said that it was now his turn to come up with a question or snappy comment to keep the discussion going. He hated it when this happened. Why couldn't the other person just keep talking? After a long pause, he came up with something. 'Who do you play for?' he asked in a tiny voice.

'Huh?'

'Who do you play for?' Sione repeated.

Daniel looked at him, puzzled. 'I play for my school. Don't you?'

Sione shook his head. He had no idea you could play rugby at your school, and certainly not regularly enough to get rep selection. He wanted to ask how long Daniel's lunchbreak was that they could fit in official matches, but his instincts told him this would not be a good follow-up question.

'I go to Barton Grammar,' Daniel added. 'What about you?'

Sione had never heard of that school. It

didn't even sound like the name of a school to him.

'Valley North?' Sione squeaked.

Daniel snorted. 'Does Valley North have lots of rugby players?'

Sione wasn't sure what Daniel was asking. 'Tonnes of people love it,' he said. 'I play on the grass pretty much every lunchtime.'

Daniel's eyebrows lowered. '*That's* how you were selected for Valley? Mucking around at lunchtime? What sort of standards do these selectors have?'

'No, no,' Sione said, waving a hand. 'I play for the Tigers in the local competition. We train at Henderson Oval near the swimming pool – you know the place? We play proper games every Saturday or Sunday. We wear uniforms and everything.'

'Huh. To tell you the truth, I was expecting everyone here to come from the schools comp. I didn't think the level of the club rugby was that high.'

Sione wasn't sure exactly what Daniel was talking about, but he wasn't going to try and guess. He had just said more words to a stranger than he ever had in his life and he felt exhausted.

To Sione, Daniel was his total opposite. His rugby experiences were of a type unknown to him, and it seemed Daniel was thinking of Sione in a similar way. It was more than awkward for him, but deep down Sione realised he was liking the idea of this trip much more now. Meeting people who lived close by but whose life stories were so different was interesting. He looked at Izzy, who smiled back. Had he heard the conversation? Sione hoped not.

Sione's very first day at rugby training felt similar to this. His dad had taken him along because Sione had said he wanted to join a team. But when he'd walked onto the field that first time, his desire was immediately replaced by fear. All the other boys already knew each other. The coach was joking around with them when his dad introduced him to the group. For some reason that had embarrassed Sione, and he had felt extra shy once he realised there were no Tongan boys on the team. No one talked to him and he didn't talk back. Everything felt foreign.

There were two reasons alone why Sione didn't ask to go home right there and then. First, he didn't want to disappoint his dad. Second, once the training drills began, Sione felt somehow free from the stares. He let his feet do the talking and he ran all over that field, chasing balls and tackling padding until he was drained of all energy. Sione made his own fun and he had never felt prouder than after that first session, gulping down some much-deserved water as his new coach sang his praises to his dad.

That was the feeling he had strived for at every training session since. 'Push yourself so that you can feel proud and enjoy that bottle of water,' was something he was continually telling himself.

'I guess they have to share things around and give everyone a go,' Daniel said, half to himself, bringing Sione back to the present. 'By giving some spots to the clubs, I mean.' He looked at Sione. 'Some people play well off the bench – that's what my dad says.'

'Some do,' Izzy said, turning to face Daniel. 'And some champions have come from the most unexpected places.'

Daniel turned around. 'Have you ever played off the bench?' he asked Izzy.

'Of course.'

'Where did you play when you were a kid? What school did you go to?'

'Minto.'

'Where's that?'

'My home, in Sydney,' Izzy answered.

'But who you play for isn't as important as *how* you play. Did you know that even players from teams at the bottom of the ladder can be selected for Australia?'

'Yeah, but it's rare,' Daniel said, now sucking on a lollipop.

'That's a lot of sugar for an athlete,' Izzy laughed. 'We won't be allowing junk food on tour, just so you know. You can only be the best you can be if you eat right.'

Daniel pulled the lollipop from his mouth with a *pop*. 'Sorry,' he said, not sounding sorry at all.

'No problem,' Izzy said, breaking into a wide smile. He looked over at Sione. 'The most important thing isn't where you started, but where you finish,' he said.

Soon after, the bus pulled up to the conference centre, which was to be the boys' home for the next two nights. It had cabins, a central building with a dining room and a big hall, and a large rugby field at the back.

'This is it, guys,' Izzy called. 'Time to get your things and get settled in. We are now officially on tour!'

DANIEL

The boys stood outside the bus in a straight line as Mary Parker went down the line, counting by twos. There were twenty boys in total. *Enough for five reserves*, Daniel thought, telling himself that there was no way he would become one of them.

'There are seven cabins for us,' Mary

announced. 'They back onto the rugby field, so we'll be nice and close to it for our training sessions. Four boys to a cabin, two cabins for the adults.

'Before we take you to your cabins, there are a few rules you need to know. There may be other groups staying here, so no loud noises or playing around the other cabins. Also, there is a games room and swimming pool in the main building, but please don't go there right now – or without one of the adults – this time is about getting settled in our rooms. In half an hour we will meet back here and talk more about the weekend.'

'Oh, and the snack machines are out of bounds, too,' Jeremy Fisk added, and all the boys groaned.

Tom Parker laughed. 'Don't worry, we will feed you very well.'

They walked in single file towards the first cabin. Some boys were passing footballs to each other as they walked.

'Eric, Joseph, Steven and TJ,' Mary said, pointing to its open door. The four boys rushed inside excitedly.

At the next cabin, another four boys cheered and high-fived when their names were read aloud. Clearly, they all knew each other. Daniel made a mental note to find out who they played for – having four from the same team went against his theory that they had shared the selections around.

Then came the third cabin. Daniel's name was called and he was inside before the other three names were even read out. As he entered, the bathroom was on his left, and in front was the main bedroom that consisted of one double bed and two sets of bunk beds. Daniel immediately threw his bag on the double bed and looked around for the TV that wasn't there.

In walked his three roommates. The first two he hadn't met yet, but the boy at the back was Sione from the bus. 'Hey, guys,' he said, nodding at the first two. 'I'm Daniel, the fly-half.'

'I'm Jake,' said the first.

'Adam,' said the second.

'How come you have the big bed?' Jake asked, pointing at Daniel's bag. He was a huge boy who looked too old for the team. He was tall and wider than both Daniel and Sione put together. His question took Daniel by surprise.

'What do you mean?' he said. 'I was here first.'

'That's just because they read out your name first,' Jake said. 'You should have waited to talk about it.'

'I was here second!' Adam said. He sprawled across the double bed, next to Daniel's bag.

'Hey, that's my bed!' Daniel snapped.

Jake and Adam laughed. Sione put his bag next to one of the bottom bunks and lay on it, his hands behind his head, waiting for the storm to blow over.

Daniel thought about his desire to be team captain and searched his mind for a clever compromise. 'How about no one gets the bed? There are enough bunks.'

Jake nodded and threw his bag on the top bunk on the other side of the room, and Adam threw his on its bottom level. Daniel turned to look at Sione, then looked at the empty bunk bed above him. *Well, at least I've got a top bunk*, he thought to himself.

The boys unpacked their belongings and placed them on the double bed. 'This can be our display table,' Daniel said. Soon, everything that the boys would be needing semi-regularly over the weekend was neatly laid out upon it instead of being tucked away in their luggage. Their four Valley jerseys were given pride of place, folded neatly along the top of the bed.

The boys then started checking out each other's football gear – the brands, colours and appearance of each boot, sock and mouthguard. Daniel found his headgear and placed it neatly on his jersey to finish his unpacking.

'You wear headgear?' Adam asked.

'Yeah, Dad wants me to wear it 'cause I took a big knock a couple of years ago,' Daniel replied. 'Anyway, it makes me stand out on the field.'

Jake picked it up and tried to slide it over his head but it didn't fit. The boys laughed as he pranced around with it on his way-too-big head.

'Lucky it's green,' Adam commented. 'Valley colours.'

Daniel shrugged. 'My school's colours are green and white. Who do you guys play for? What school?'

'I go to St Christopher's,' Adam said proudly.

'I'm at Queens,' Jake said.

'Who do you play for again?' Daniel asked Sione.

Sione sat up and took the headphones out of his ears. 'Huh?'

Daniel turned back to the others. 'He doesn't go to a rugby school. He plays for a club – the Tigers?'

'Yeah.' Sione nodded and pointed at his pile of training gear on the double bed. Everything was orange and black.

'Cool,' Adam said.

Jake gestured to the wall behind Sione. 'What's that?' he asked.

'Nothing,' Sione said quickly.

A folded piece of paper was stuck to the wall. Jake walked over to Sione's bed to take a closer look. 'It's the email Izzy sent to all of us.'

'You kept it?' Adam said, laughing.

Daniel smirked. 'We all got that. I didn't even keep a copy.'

'I know, right?' The other two laughed.

Sione shrugged, his cheeks flushed. 'I like it,' he said, softly but defiantly.

The boys stood outside listening to the plan for the rest of their stay. They had free time before dinner, followed by team-building exercises in the hall. Daniel grunted. That didn't seem interesting at all.

'After that,' Tom announced, 'Izzy is going to show you some rugby video clips and discuss them with you.'

'Woo!' Daniel howled. That was more his style!

Tom threw him a warning look. 'Tomorrow is training all day, starting after breakfast. I'll tell you more about that later but there's all sorts of things planned. We'll have a practice game or two on Monday before we head to the airport.'

'When do we have to go to bed tonight?' asked one of the boys.

'Lights out at nine-thirty sharp.'

'What?' Daniel exclaimed, horrified. 'That's way early!'

'Trust me – with all the work we have to do tomorrow, you'll need the rest,' Izzy said from behind the crowd. Everyone turned to face him. 'I can't have you guys falling asleep on the field, can I?' he added, laughing heartily.

Daniel hung his head. This camp was starting to sound more like a punishment than a reward.

'Remember that we aren't here to have a party,' Jeremy added. 'You are all being taught the importance of teamwork and commitment – qualities you need if you are to be a rugby champion.'

Daniel frowned, confused. The messages he was getting on this trip about rugby were nothing like his dad's advice.

At dinner, Daniel sat with Adam and Jake and they talked the whole time about their schools, teams and the amazing tries they'd scored. Afterwards, Tom, Mary and

Izzy took the boys through a series of team-building games. For some of the activities, Daniel was paired up with Sione, who, in his opinion, was the worst teammate *ever*. When Daniel was blindfolded and being led around an obstacle course, Sione kept bumping him into things. When they had to answer trivia questions, Sione always got them wrong. When they had to solve problems, Sione just got confused.

Each activity scored the partnerships points, and after finishing last in the rankings for the night, Daniel had had enough. 'This isn't rugby,' he complained loudly.

Izzy sighed. 'No, it isn't,' he said. 'But if you can't work together off the field, how will you cooperate when you're on it?'

Daniel glared at Sione. It was a good thing he'd be far away on the wing and out of trouble.

SIONE

Sione was roused early the next morning by the sound of kookaburras singing outside his cabin. He tucked his hands behind his head and watched the room gradually brighten as the sun's rays slipped inside. He lay there for what felt like hours, listening to the mattress above him creak with Daniel's every move and Jake's snores.

Sione wasn't sure why everyone always wanted the top bunk; he preferred the bottom. It was like a private room, with a roof and a wall. He turned to the wall and looked at the email from Izzy. He didn't know why he'd hung onto it; all he knew was it made him feel special and want to play well.

Perhaps it was also a source of comfort. Sione was feeling more and more out of place on the camp. Last night, many of the boys – including Jake, Adam and Daniel – had dressed up in nice clothes for dinner. They'd done their hair and sprayed deodorant. It was like they all knew they should do it, while Sione just walked into the dining room in his tracksuit. No one said anything, but Sione knew what they were all thinking.

All they ate was plain old spaghetti bolognaise, but the others had treated it like a meal in a fancy restaurant. *Is this a chance to learn and play great rugby, or a popularity contest?* Sione had wondered.

And the less said about the team games and training videos the better. Daniel had spent the night complaining about how inferior a partner Sione was. Sione had been hurt and confused by it all. Daniel had been the one who seemed to sabotage all their attempts to succeed, but by vocalising that Sione was to blame, everyone had joined in with Daniel and pointed fingers at him. He had only wanted to have some fun, but as soon as it was clear they weren't going to win the events, Daniel just gave up.

During the video session, Izzy had shown some famous tries from the last couple of World Cups. After each clip, Izzy asked the boys how the try was scored. Daniel would call out the answer every time, yelling things like, 'The cut-out pass threw the defence off guard' or 'The brute strength of the forwards pushed him over'. Each time Izzy would say that he was partly correct, but that it was teamwork that had really resulted in the tries.

'The whole team has to work together to be on the same page,' Izzy had said, 'and each member can't be worried about taking the limelight for themselves.'

Sione had loved this lesson while Daniel kept snorting his disagreement, even after Izzy had pointed out how the things that players without the ball were doing affected the player running with it.

Sione was getting cross just thinking about it. He got out of bed and jumped in the shower. By the time Sione had left the bathroom, washed and dressed, it was still an hour before breakfast and the other three boys were still asleep. Quietly, Sione grabbed his hoodie off the double bed and left the room to go for a walk.

The crisp morning air was refreshing and Sione smiled at the way the bright sunshine made the leaves in the trees sparkle. The kookaburras' laughing had been replaced by other birdsongs now, and Sione shielded his eyes from the sun with his hood and set out for the rugby field.

Before every Tigers game, Sione liked to walk a couple of laps of the field, thinking about the game and how it might go. With the first training session only a couple of hours away, Sione wasn't sure he'd get the opportunity, so now seemed like a good time to get to know the posts, line markings and pitch before he would be expected to perform upon it.

He walked between two cabins and through some bushes before emerging onto a field. It was a simple rectangle of grass with the familiar white posts at each end of it. Bordered all around by trees and cabins, the space seemed enclosed – private and special.

But Sione wasn't alone. At the far end of the pitch, he spied a familiar figure sprinting back and forth between the tryline and the 22-yard line. It was Izzy, in a green-and-gold training top and white boots, huffing and puffing. Sione watched from a distance as Izzy gulped down some water before switching to a jumping and skipping drill, moving up and down the touchline. He watched in silence for a long time, half-thinking the right thing to do would be to give his coach some privacy, the other half wanting to learn how champions train.

Sione was proud that he had Izzy Folau as a mentor – someone who led by example, rather than with hollow words or power.

When Izzy had finished, he stretched on the grass and finished the rest of his water.

'Oh, hey, Sione,' he said with a wave, finally noticing his single spectator.

'Hey,' Sione replied. 'Sorry.'

'There's no need to apologise. You can join me tomorrow morning, if you like.'

Sione's jaw dropped. 'Um, okay,' he said.

Izzy walked over. 'I want to keep up with my training, and mornings are really the only time I have on tour. How have you found the camp so far?'

'Okay,' Sione replied. He hoped he didn't sound ungrateful.

'I'm sure it will be great fun, but I know how hard it is to start somewhere new,' Izzy said, wiping his forehead with a towel. 'Did you know rugby union is my third sport?'

Sione nodded.

'Each time I've faced a new challenge it has been really hard, but I've had great times and learnt so much. I think you will, too.'

Sione smiled. 'That's why my aunty likes you so much,' he said.

Izzy laughed. 'Next time you speak to her, tell your aunty that I'm very flattered.'

After a hearty breakfast, the boys hit the rugby field for the first time as a group. Most boys came with the expectation they would be doing skills training or position work, but the first session was purely based on fitness. Izzy took the boys through a full warm-up routine, a set of runs and finished off with a beep test. At the very mention of the beep test, most of the other players groaned, Daniel moaning the loudest of all. Sione, too shy to say he didn't know what a beep test was, listened intently to Izzy's explanation. He learnt that this test was made up of a series of back-and-forth sprints that are timed with beeps. Runners were given less and less time to complete each run the further they progressed. If a boy didn't make his mark before the beep sounded, he was knocked out of the test and given a score.

With each turn, Sione pictured Izzy earlier that morning, pushing himself to do his best, even though no one was watching. Sione was so deep in thought he was oblivious to the other boys dropping out around him, to

Daniel's complaints when he was knocked out, and to the fact that, eventually, the group of runners had dwindled down to just him and TJ.

Cheers rang out after every completed lap, rousing Sione from his thoughts. He couldn't believe it. Boys were clapping for him, encouraging him to keep going.

Then TJ was gone and it was just him left. How he made each mark before the beeps, Sione didn't know. Each sprint was now incredibly fast and his heart was beating rapidly. Worse than that, though, was the heavy feeling in his thighs and calves. *Just one more*, he thought. *No regrets.*

Beep . . . beep . . .

'Just one more!'

Cheers rained down when the current speed was announced. Sione collapsed on the ground, hands patting him from every direction.

'Try and stand up, Sione,' he heard Izzy say, as if from the other end of a tunnel. 'You'll recover quicker. Hands on your head.'

Sione did as he was told. He was shocked at his ability and proud of his drive. There would be no regrets for him today. Adam handed him a bottle of water and it tasted like liquid gold.

There was a break for morning tea and a little free time before everyone was expected back on the field for some drills. The others continued to congratulate Sione, though he tried to keep a low profile. As great as the beep test had been, he knew that the next session, when he would actually have to show some playing skills, was the real test.

The boys were split into backs and forwards. As there were a few too many players, Izzy planned to interchange them regularly. Due to his morning's efforts, Sione was picked to be left wing first. The drill was set up — a simple one so Izzy could see the team in motion. The forwards had to form a scrum around a scrum machine as the backs stretched out along the field behind them.

Daniel found the ball and smiled so wide Sione could see it from the other side of the field. Had he practised this recently? Daniel threw the ball to Harrison, the scrum-half, and gave him a high five.

Sione watched as Harrison fed the ball into the semi-scrum. He enjoyed these moments of solitude on the field, all the way out near the far touchline on his own. He set himself, watching and waiting . . .

And then the ball came free. The backs quickly advanced in a line, ensuring that they didn't move in front of the players to their right. The ball flew along the row of backs. Soon it would be in Sione's hands.

Tom, Mary, Jeremy and Izzy were applauding the ball's progress from some-where behind him. It was now with the boy at outside centre. Sione was next.

The ball was passed to Sione, but with much more force than he was expecting. It came at him like a spinning dart. It went through his hands and punched him in the chest with its point.

Sione exhaled and stumbled to the ground. 'Ugh!'

The ball bounced over the touchline and into a bush. The other nineteen boys groaned, and Sione's stomach plummeted.

DANIEL

The day before had been extremely tiring but lots of fun. They had done so much work on the field that Daniel had fallen asleep before lights out, and it had been a great feeling to wake up on Monday morning, knowing that his deep rest had been well deserved.

The Sunday highlights for Daniel would definitely have been the amazing roast dinner and movie night, but the display of his bunk mate on the training pitch was something he couldn't get out of his head.

Sione had been popular in the morning when all they had been doing was running. But when the rugby balls came out, Daniel saw it was a different story. Sione had totally fallen apart. He couldn't catch anything, and most repetitions and drills stopped short whenever he went near the play.

Daniel wasn't sure why Sione had been so nervous. After training was finally over, Sione had disappeared to the shower but Daniel had stayed out and practised his goal kicking, just as he did after every session. Izzy congratulated him on his extra effort, which filled him with pride.

When he had eventually returned to their cabin, Sione had been even quieter than usual. Daniel supposed he had learnt that schoolboy rugby was better.

Now it was Monday and, for Daniel, the day had an aura of excitement about it. Not only were they heading to the airport after lunch, but Izzy had scheduled practice matches for the morning session. Daniel was really looking forward to it so he could properly show off his captaincy skills.

After breakfast, the boys gathered around Izzy at the halfway line. Sione stood back from the main group as he listened.

Daniel wanted him to stand with them, the way a teammate should. *You've got to learn to take this game by the horns, Sione*, Daniel wanted to say. *Don't be afraid or you'll never get better.*

Sione's eyes met Daniel's for a split second before he looked down again.

'So this is how it's going to work,' Izzy began. 'It's ten to a side, with twenty-minute halves. After one game we will have a break, mix you up and go again. With less players, some of you will have to play altered positions – the scrum will be smaller, the back line shorter – but you'll have more space and time to do all your magic tricks.' Izzy winked at Daniel, who attached his chin strap to show he was ready. 'Show me everything you've got, and remember to have some fun!'

118

The boys were then split into two even teams, with Sione and Daniel on opposite sides. Daniel gathered all his teammates around him. 'Good luck, guys,' he said. 'I'm the only kicker here, so I'll do all that. We don't really know each other yet, so we may make mistakes, but don't worry. Listen to my instructions if you aren't sure what we should do.'

Jake and Adam rolled their eyes but said nothing.

In a moment, they were standing along the halfway line as Daniel prepared to kick off. Izzy blew the whistle, and Daniel kicked the ball with pinpoint accuracy towards Sione. He was standing in the right corner of the field, and as the ball screamed towards him, his legs seemed to wobble like jelly and his arms awkwardly shot up to try and catch the ball.

'Catch it!' his teammates cried.

The ball sank and, instead of taking it on the full, Sione decided to let it bounce first. But it didn't come to him. The ball hit the grass and shot off at a right angle, over the touchline. There would now be a line-out, just metres from Daniel's tryline.

Players came over to pat Daniel on the back, congratulating him on the kick. With giant Jake on their side, the line-out was theirs for the taking. No one went to congratulate Sione this time.

Jake won the line-out, jumping high with Adam's support, and after a beautiful, long set-up pass from Daniel, TJ scored a try under the posts. Daniel kicked the conversion easily, bringing the score to 7–0 within a couple of minutes.

'Don't worry, B Team,' Izzy called, 'this is just a practice match and the scores don't count. I want to hear more talk, though, okay?'

There *was* more talk from the other team after that, but from what Daniel could hear, it was all directed at Sione and it didn't sound positive.

As the game continued, Daniel noticed that most of the defensive pressure was aimed at him and he loved that. Yes, it made things more difficult to have multiple, big forwards bearing down on you at every moment, but it meant that they were afraid of him, that he was playing well. As Daniel's dad often said, it was the ultimate compliment to have a team worried about you.

At the end of the forty minutes, Izzy began by reminding everyone that the score was irrelevant and he hadn't taken notice. But Daniel had. His team had won 31–5, with Daniel kicking five out of five attempts and setting up three tries. Tim, the goal kicker on the other side, had missed his only attempt. Daniel was more than pleased with his performance.

With fewer players, there hadn't been as much tackling, rucking and mauling as one would normally expect in a game but everyone was still feeling banged up and ready for a rest. The only thing that kept them wanting to play the second game was the desire to impress.

After a cool-down, sandwiches and then another warm-up, the boys positioned themselves on the two sides of the field for the second practice match. This time Daniel and Sione were on the same team.

'If the ball is kicked to you,' Daniel said in Sione's direction, 'either catch it or get out of the way so someone else can.'

Sione hung his head and walked over to his side of the field.

There was no pep talk this time. Daniel was sure everyone knew to follow his lead. But before kicking off, he saw Izzy talking to Sione quietly. Daniel grimaced and looked away. *I should be the one getting the attention,* he thought. *Can't Izzy see all the good things I'm doing?*

The game began and the teams were clearly more evenly matched this time. There was no score in the first half, just lots of bumps and bruises as players struggled to gain some kind of advantage. At one point the ball was stuck in a small zone of Daniel's half for what seemed like forever. In an attempt to break the deadlock after his teammates had regained possession of the ball from a furious rucking contest, Daniel screamed for it and promptly kicked the ball high and down field – about forty metres towards his scoring end – and out of bounds. Even Izzy cheered him after that.

The ball came back into play, was passed down the back line, and when Sione actually managed to receive a pass, it looked certain the team would score. Sione broke expertly through two defenders and was clear, but instead of heading straight for the tryline, he cut back inside towards the goalposts. There, he found Jake waiting for him.

Sione went down and the scoring opportunity disappeared. He placed the ball behind him in the tackle and Daniel picked it up, passing it to Adam, who passed it on to TJ. It was he, with the defence in disarray, who scored in the corner on the other side of the pitch.

'Look, see that?' Daniel shouted at Sione in frustration. 'Next time, just go for the line. Sometimes there's no room to be fancy.'

Sione clenched his teeth and stared at Daniel. 'I was trying to help the team, okay? You aren't the coach! Just leave me alone!'

The other players were stunned speechless. It was the most they'd heard Sione say, and certainly the loudest his voice had ever been these past three days.

Izzy ran over, a concerned look on his face. 'Hey, guys, calm down! What's up?'

'He keeps picking on me,' Sione said, hating the whine in his voice.

'No, I don't. I'm just trying to help,' Daniel shot back, shaking his head.

'I'm sure you are just trying to help,' Izzy said gently, 'but remember that Sione is trying his best. He wants to play well.'

Daniel knew Izzy was right, but it didn't stop him from feeling frustrated. He wanted Sione to focus and to play like a rep. He had only been trying to wake him up.

'Sorry,' Sione said softly. 'I'm just stressed out about not playing well.'

'I'm sorry too,' Daniel said grudgingly. 'I need to say things nicer, I guess.'

The ball was thrown from somewhere and bounced at Daniel's feet. He took it and set up his conversion kick, glad to get out of the awkward conversation. It was a tough kick from all the way out near touch. It got enough height but didn't move in the air nearly as much as it needed to, sailing well clear of the nearest post.

Daniel kicked his tee in disgust. Arguing with Sione must have put him off. He stared at him in frustration. He wasn't sorry at all. Why was Sione even on this team?

The second half was as tight as the first, but both teams managed tries. The tie was broken in the eighteenth minute by Sione, who scored a lucky try under the posts. Daniel didn't watch, but he did kick the conversion so hard it got stuck high in a tree.

'All right, let's end the game there,' Izzy said. 'You all deserve an early mark. Hit the showers and then we'll have lunch. We'll discuss these games as a group after that.'

While most of the boys were revelling in the experience, Daniel felt nothing but anger and frustration.

'Daniel, Sione,' Izzy called out before they could leave. Both boys trudged over to him, dreading what was to come. 'There's no need to look so down, guys – you both played great, and I'm glad you're on the Valley team. I think this is going to be a terrific tour.'

'But?' Daniel said.

Izzy smiled. 'There are no buts. I've changed sports a few times, and every time

I did there were people who weren't happy. Without meaning to, I upset fans, the media and, worst of all, my teammates. Each time I had to walk into a change room filled with people I didn't know to play a game I wasn't too sure about. I found it hard to be happy and relaxed sometimes, but I did my best to make it work. I trained, I was nice to people, I was a good teammate. You know why?'

'Why?' Daniel asked.

'If I didn't, I might as well have gone home. It's the same for you guys. If you can't chill out, have fun and be proud of your achievements, then you might as well think about going home. Though, I'm pretty sure neither of you want to do that.'

Daniel laughed at the idea. 'No way,' he said.

Sione exhaled loudly, and Daniel and Izzy both turned to look at him. As frustrated as Daniel had felt with Sione, he didn't want to hear him say he'd had enough of the tour.

'I don't know how to get home from here, anyway,' Sione said after a long pause, and all three of them burst into laughter.

With that, Daniel and Sione walked back to their cabin side by side, a fresh start in the air.

SIONE

You might as well go home. The words echoed in Sione's head as he showered and changed. He could hear the other boys in his room joking around. Part of him wished he was friendly enough with them to join in. The other half of him wished they'd just go away.

He got his mobile out of the bag under his bed, sneakily sliding it into a pocket in his track pants before leaving the room. He knew that if the others saw his beat-up, old pre-paid phone it would just be one more thing for Daniel to put him down about.

Sione walked back to the rugby field. It was five minutes before lunch, so he didn't have long. Quickly, he dialled the only phone number he knew off by heart.

'Hi, it's me,' he said when his aunty answered.

'It's Sione! Mele, Vili, come say hello! You're okay, right?' she said.

'Yes,' Sione answered. It felt kind of weird talking to her. He hadn't been gone from home very long, but it felt like his family was in another country. He could imagine Mele hopping down the hallway towards the phone and he felt so homesick he almost cried.

'Hi, Sione!' his sister yelled, breathing heavily into the phone.

Sione smiled. 'Hey.'

'Guess what? Dad said I can get a puppy! Soon, when I'm ten.'

Sione laughed. 'But that's, like, six years away.'

'It's soon!' his little sister insisted.

'Sione doesn't want to talk about puppies,' he could hear his aunt say in the background. 'Give the phone to your dad.'

'Bye, Sione!' Mele called before the slow, familiar voice of his father took over.

'How's it going, son? Have you played yet?' his dad asked.

'Yeah, just training and practice matches, though.'

'Going good?'

'I guess.'

'Good boy. Make sure you have fun. We'll be there to see you at the Championships in a couple of weeks, yeah? Terry's coming, too.'

'Okay.'

'Call if you need.'

'Yep.'

'We're very proud of you, Sione,' his aunt said. 'Just do your best and remember to have fun – you'll never forget this experience.'

How did Aunty do that? She always seemed

to know what Sione needed to hear. 'Okay,' he said before saying goodbye.

Sione returned the phone to his pocket and wiped his eyes. Somehow, that three-minute phone call had given him his strength back. His on-field mistakes seemed miles away. He ran back to his cabin, grabbed his favourite cap and hurried off after his teammates.

That afternoon, after a final chat from Izzy about the team, it was time to pack and head to the airport. Sione couldn't wait for the next stage of their journey. This weekend had been tough, but Sione could already see it had been worth it. *Who knows?* he thought. *I might even become friends with some of the boys.*

While the others took their time packing, Sione decided to make one last visit to the rugby field. As he passed between the last row of cabins, the kookaburras began laughing and, once again, there was a lone figure training on the pitch.

But it wasn't Izzy this time, it was Daniel. He was practising his goal kicking in his regular clothes and football boots. Sione watched him place the ball on the tee before looking. Their eyes met, and Daniel froze. Sione didn't know what to do. Should he leave? He certainly didn't feel like walking a lap of the field now, but something inside told him to walk over instead.

'You're a good goal kicker,' he said. They were the only words he could think of that he knew wouldn't make Daniel angry.

'Thanks,' Daniel replied. 'You're a great runner.'

Sione was stunned. He didn't know what he was expecting, but that definitely wasn't it. 'Thanks.'

They both stood there saying nothing for a long time, until Sione surprised himself by being the one who broke the silence. 'When did you start playing rugby?' he asked.

'When I was six, I think,' Daniel answered. 'We started doing it for PE at school, and when I was a bit older I started playing on a real team.'

'Hey, same as me!' Sione said, perking up. 'Dad took me to the local club when I was six. It wasn't proper rugby – it was some kid's version. But, yeah, been playing ever since.'

'That was at the Tigers?'

Sione shook his head. 'We move, like, every year. That was in a whole other town.'

'Oh,' Daniel said, kicking the grass. 'It's weird. If I didn't go to Barton, we'd probably be playing on the same team, I reckon.'

'Maybe.'

'My dad loves rugby. He's wanted me to play ever since I was born, so I would be playing somewhere, I know it.'

'That's like my dad, too,' Sione said, breaking into a smile. 'If it wasn't for him I wouldn't be playing.'

'Maybe I could come watch the Tigers play one day,' Daniel said.

'Yeah, and I could come see you play too.'

A heavy footfall sounded behind them, and they both turned to see Izzy approaching.

'Hey, guys,' he said, 'want to practise some passing before we have to go?'

'Sure!' the boys said in unison.

They stood in a triangle, passing the ball around, first in one direction and then the other. In the trees behind them, kookaburras called and a plane flew by overhead.

DANIEL

Daniel climbed onto the bus and sat beside Sione. 'This will be easier than talking across the aisle,' he said casually.

Sione nodded, a smile curling his lips.

Daniel looked past Sione and out the window as the bus rumbled along the driveway. The trees and buildings of the conference centre that had become so familiar so quickly were soon left behind. He was surprised to find he was sad to leave. The thing was, he realised, this weekend hadn't just been about rugby. He'd met his new team, he'd had fun on the field for the first time in ages and he'd made new friends.

In a few hours, the team would be on their way to the Gold Coast to continue their training and play exhibition games against local teams. It would provide them with a much tougher opposition than playing intra-team games could ever produce. *Plus*, Daniel told himself, *Izzy probably thinks going on a trip will help us to bond as a team.* He remembered what Jake had said about a hundred times that morning – 'As long as

I get to go to a theme park, I'll be happy' –
and chuckled.

Sione and Daniel talked about everything
but rugby on the way to the airport. They
told each other about where they lived, what
their school uniforms looked like, and their
families. They even discovered they had one
major thing in common, but it was something
neither boy wanted to talk about just yet.

When the bus pulled up at the airport,
everyone cheered and clamoured to get off
the bus. All except for Sione, who slunk down
low in his seat.

'What's wrong?' Daniel asked. 'Don't like
flying?'

Sione shook his head. 'I haven't been on a
plane since I was a baby.'

Daniel was slightly taken aback, but he tried to not let his surprise show. 'Don't worry, it's nothing,' he said. 'You'll probably get your own TV. They give you food and we'll go up even higher than the clouds – it's heaps of fun!'

'Really?' Sione said, sounding unconvinced.

'Yeah. Come on, I'll sit next to you on the plane, too.'

'Okay,' Sione replied, standing up. 'You can have the window seat this time.'

They walked out of the bus together, and Izzy smiled at them as they walked past. Then, all three said thank you and goodbye to their driver and they walked inside the terminal.

'My uncle is an air steward,' Daniel said. 'He's been all over the world millions of times. I think it would be a cool job, but Dad says I won't have much time for a job like that with uni and playing rugby for Australia.' Daniel could see Sione squirm at this and decided to change tack. 'Look, here's where we check in our bags, then we go through the security area over there and then wait at our gate to board the plane. Maybe we could go and look at the shops and stuff first. It's easy. It's just like a huge train station.'

And it did go easily. They were soon on the plane, waiting for lift-off.

'It's very noisy in here,' Sione observed, looking around the cabin.

Daniel nodded. 'It's normal. You'll get used to it – it's the engines or the air systems or something. Try to block it out. That's a trick we'll have to get used to if we are going to be playing lots of games in front of huge, unfriendly crowds!'

Sione laughed and tried to settle in, exploring the in-flight entertainment options. He watched the flight crew perform the safety instructions as the plane drove around the tarmac and then . . . Wow!

The speed of the plane was tremendous as it shot forwards. The rumbling from the engines and wheels along the tarmac was deafening. Just when Daniel wondered how much more of the runway there could be, the plane became noticeably lighter and the vibrations coming up through the floor disap-peared. They were in the air!

Daniel turned to Sione and found that he was smiling so wide that Daniel could have counted all of his teeth.

'Wooooohooooo!' they both cried as the plane climbed higher. This was as good as any theme-park ride!

Izzy's familiar voice filled the air. 'Valley! Valley! Valley!' he chanted.

'Oi! Oi! Oi!' the boys yelled back.

Daniel and Sione turned to each other and grinned. This was it. It was really happening. They were representative rugby players, on their way to unknown adventures with their team.

SIONE TAITO

POSITION: Wing

SCHOOL: Valley North

TEAM: The Tigers

LOVES TO: Watch Izzy Folau play on TV

Picked to play for the Valley team on the wing, Sione has many attributes that good wingers need. He is fast, fit and able to find a gap within any line of defence. At first, Sione wasn't sure if playing on a rep team was the right fit for him, but since finding his feet with Valley, he has become more comfortable with his selection.

Soft-spoken Sione does all his 'talking' on the rugby field, where he strives to play with the enthusiasm and happiness of his hero, Izzy Folau. Sione plays for the Tigers in his local competition. There, he has excelled and become what many rugby fans might call a 'try-scoring machine', though those are words he would never use to describe himself.

DANIEL MASTERS

POSITION: Fly-half

SCHOOL: Barton Grammar

TEAM: Barton Grammar

LOVES TO: Kick a match-winning goal

Daniel plays for Valley at the vital position of fly-half. As he directs the back line on the field, he also tries hard to lead by example off the field. Daniel's ultimate dream is to captain Australia at the Rugby World Cup. Sometimes his dedication and desire to win get in the way of having a good time, but with Valley, he is learning to do both.

Daniel is also a terrific goal kicker who is never happier than after kicking one hundred per cent of his attempts in a match. His success comes from the extra hard work he puts in after training and on his days off. If there ever was a boy who loved his rugby, it's Daniel. Possibly the most passionate rugby player in the world after Izzy Folau, Daniel never stops giving his all.

VALLEY TEAM

Name: Daniel Masters

Position: Fly-half

Plays for: Barton Grammar

Known for: His accurate goal kicking

Greatest moment: Leading his team to an undefeated season

Name: Sione 'the Eel' Taito

Position: Wing

Plays for: The Tigers

Known for: Weaving through defenders

Greatest moment: Being selected for the Valley rep team

Name: Theo 'TJ' Jones

Position: Fullback

Plays for: Grantham Boys

Known for: Catching high balls under pressure

Greatest moment: Scoring three tries in a grand final

Name: Steven Hendricks

Position: Wing

Plays for: The Bears

Known for: His courage under pressure

Greatest moment: Scoring a try in his first game

Name: Eric Le

Position: Centre

Plays for: Saxby Prep

Known for: Being selected for Valley in his first year playing rugby

Greatest moment: Scoring a hundred-metre try

Name: Joseph Rosenberg

Position: Centre

Plays for: Saxby Prep

Known for: His ability to set up tries

Greatest moment: Putting five other teammates on the scoreboard in one game

Name: Harrison Gordon

Position: Scrum-half

Plays for: Bunyan Bunyips

Known for: His leadership at the scrum

Greatest moment: Winning his team's Best Player trophy two years in a row

Name: Derek 'the Ringmaster' Ngo

Position: Wing

Plays for: Clifton Grammar

Known for: Running rings around the opposition

Greatest moment: Being promoted from the D Team to the A Team at school within two weeks

Name: Ty Fennelly

Position: Fullback

Plays for: St Francis's

Known for: His long kick returns

Greatest moment: Scoring twenty-five points in one match

Name: Jake Hunter

Position: Prop

Plays for: Queens

Known for: His strong tackling

Greatest moment: Playing every minute of every game last season

Name: Benny Simons

Position: Prop

Plays for: Queens

Known for: Pushing opposition teams back in the scrum

Greatest moment: Being selected for two different rep teams in two different states

Name: Adam El-Attar

Position: Hooker

Plays for: St Christopher's

Known for: His jumping in the line-out

Greatest moment: Making thirty tackles in one game

Name: Tim Broadbent

Position: Second row

Plays for: The Saints

Known for: His goal kicking

Greatest moment: His tackle in extra time that saved his team's season

Name: Patrick Mulholland

Position: Second row

Plays for: The Saints

Known for: Taking on any opponent, no matter how big

Greatest moment: Chasing down an opponent from twenty metres behind, then tackling him into touch

Name: Terry 'Tezza' Williams

Position: Flanker

Plays for: The Bears

Known for: His speed down the blind side

Greatest moment: Scoring a try in every game last season

Name: Zach Smith

Position: Flanker

Plays for: St Francis's

Known for: His ability to play as a forward or back

Greatest moment: Being his team's captain and also its youngest player

Name: Nathan Davidson

Position: Number-eight

Plays for: Clifton Grammar

Known for: His seemingly unlimited energy

Greatest moment: Regularly landing twenty-metre-long passes to teammates

Name: Kane Williams

Position: Utility-forward

Plays for: The Saints

Known for: His accurate kicking for touch

Greatest moment: Playing in every forward position last season

Name: Sean de Groot

Position: Utility-forward

Plays for: Clifton Grammar

Known for: His 'never give up' attitude

Greatest moment: Winning a grand final with an extra-time try

Name: Kian Hardy

Position: Utility-forward

Plays for: Clifton Grammar

Known for: Always walking off the field covered in mud

Greatest moment: He has played for three Premiership-winning teams

ISRAEL FOLAU

NICKNAME: Izzy

BORN: 3 April 1989 in Minto, NSW

HEIGHT: 195 cm

WEIGHT: 103 kg

POSITION: Fullback

TEAM: NSW Waratahs, Australian Wallabies

IZZY'S CAREER

2007/08: NRL Melbourne Storm

2007–2009: Australian Kangaroos

2008–2010: Queensland Maroons

2009/10: NRL Brisbane Broncos

2010: NRL All Stars

2011/2012: AFL Greater Western Sydney Giants

2013–present: NSW Waratahs

2013–present: Australian Wallabies

IZZY'S TRAINING TIPS: PASSING

You may think that passing a ball is as simple as tossing it in the air in the direction of one of your teammates. However, to become a great passer, there is a lot to think about before you let the ball leave your fingers.

As you pass a ball, hold it with both hands. Use your hand furthest away from your target to push the ball, and the other one to guide it. Your hands should end up in the direction of your target after letting go.

A successful rugby pass must be of the correct strength and height and be on target.

TARGET: Remember to look at the player you wish to pass the ball to and swing your arms in their direction. If your pass is not accurate, it may not be caught.

STRENGTH: If your pass is too soft it will not reach your target. Too hard, and it will hit them too vigorously. Practise passing from different distances to learn how hard your passes should be.

HEIGHT: This is similar to your strength. If your pass is too high or too low it will be difficult to catch and may be dropped.

Did you know that waiting to pass can be just as important as passing the ball? Sometimes, players want to get rid of the ball as soon as they gain possession of it, but take that split second before you pass to consider your options. Consider who you are going to pass to and whether they are ready to receive it.

Why not try this training drill to improve your passing strength?

Stand a metre away from your partner. Pass the ball to them, remembering correct positioning and technique. If they catch it at their chest, your partner should pass the ball back to you. Whenever both of you successfully pass and receive the ball, both of you can then take a step back. Now the passing distance is greater. How far can you go?

COLLECT THE SERIES

OUT NOW